EPIC NEW ZEALAND ADVENTURERS

MARIA GILL AND MARCO IVANCIC

upstart press

A catalogue record for this book is available from the National Library of New Zealand

ISBN 978-1-77694-012-7

An Upstart Press Book
Published in 2023 by Upstart Press Ltd
26 Greenpark Road
Penrose, Auckland 1061, New Zealand

Design and layout by redinc Book design, www.redinc.co.nz
Printed in China by Everbest Printing Ltd

CONTENTS

INTRODUCTION

Aotearoa New Zealand is a land of adventurers, from the first explorers sailing here in their waka from islands in the Pacific, European explorers wishing to draw a global map, and Māori and European settlers traversing the mountainous regions of New Zealand. But historians have already written much about those explorers. This book includes the epic journeys of more recent New Zealand explorers.

A book of adventurers couldn't be without **Jean Batten**, the daredevil pilot who set world records flying from England to New Zealand. It also couldn't be without **Sir Edmund Hillary,** as he and Tenzing Norgay were the first to climb the world's highest peak, Mt Everest. But you know those stories. Instead, Jean's escapade is about her riskiest flight ever: the trip that nearly ended her life many times. Sir Edmund Hillary's story is about the race to the South Pole, a risky expedition across crevices and lumpy Antarctic ice in a red tractor.

The next eight stories are about adventurers you should know about and perhaps don't.

- **Paul Caffyn**, the Australian-born, New Zealand-based kayaker, circumnavigated Australia in a kayak. You must have great stamina and determination to do that!
- **Matahi Brightwell** sailed from Tahiti to New Zealand in a traditional voyaging waka in tumultuous seas and shark-infested waters.
- **Lydia Bradey** climbed Mt Everest without oxygen and was the first woman to do so. How brave was that?

- **Helen Thayer** had climbed the highest mountains and traversed the hottest and coldest countries in the world. Then she battled polar bears, cyclonic winds and near-starvation to reach her goal of being the first woman to trek solo to the Magnetic North Pole. National Geographic named her one of the greatest explorers of the twentieth century!
- **Lisa Tamati** walked through the forbidden military zone in Egypt's Western Desert and nearly died in the process.
- **Cam McLeay** and **Garth MacIntyre** wanted to find the source of the Nile River. They encountered crocodiles, hippos and a dangerous rebel force.
- Fourteen-year-old **Laura Dekker** sailed around the world on her own in search of adventure!
- Lastly, **Mark Watson** and **Hana Black** cycled from Alaska to South America, facing grizzly bears, scorpions and an earthquake, not to mention the pandemic that swept the world.

What compels a person to travel around or through a country or continent alone? Is it to test themselves, a will to be the first, or an urge to set a world record?

For Lisa Tamati, it was to prove to herself she wasn't a failure. Her father had always pushed Lisa and her brothers to do their best, and she felt she hadn't lived up to his expectations. Laura Dekker had grown up living with her family on a boat and sailing the world. Going to school every day back in Holland wasn't challenging enough. She wanted to see more of the world. While Matahi Brightwell wanted to show everyone that he could voyage using only traditional sailing and navigational methods from one Pacific country to New Zealand.

Whatever their reasons, it takes pure grit, perseverance and survival know-how to make it to the end. If you fancy yourself as an adventurer one day, look on pages 46–47 to find tips on how to keep safe.

Brace yourself for these incredible feats of bravery.

Epic adventures await you...

JEAN BATTEN – A NEAR FATAL FLIGHT

London–Darwin–Sydney–Darwin–Auckland, 12 April to 29 April 1935

Jean Batten had just beaten English pilot Amy Johnson's world-record flight from England to Australia by five days in 1935 and was ready to break another record. She wanted to be the first woman to fly solo from England to Australia and back. She had the Gypsy Moth airplane's engine overhauled in Sydney. But when she set off from Darwin airport on 12 April, she had a nagging feeling something wasn't right.

Three hours out of Darwin, while looking down at the red haze from a dust storm and getting the occasional glimpse of the blue sea, Jean's engine spluttered. She stared at the controls. *What was happening?* Then it coughed again, shaking the entire plane. But this time, it didn't spring back to life. It went silent. Deadly silent. The engine had stopped. The plane glided downwards.

Jean's eyes darted over the controls. How could she fix it? She had only fifteen minutes before she'd descend into the ocean. It couldn't be a shortage of petrol in the main gravity tank, as she'd just pumped some up. Jean jerked the throttle back and forth, hoping the engine would kick-start itself. Nothing happened. That's when a sense of helplessness swept over her as the sea came closer.

Jean yanked at the throttle again, moving it up and down. Do something! she raged at the engine. Within minutes, she was in the pink clouds before dropping below them. The altimeter unwound from 1200 to 1000 and then 900 metres. Air whooshed past as she dropped lower and lower.

The wide expanse of the Timor Sea stretched before her. She dreaded capsizing into the ocean. There was no lifejacket, life raft or radio on board to help her if she did. Pumping the throttle produced no results, so she left it wide open. Perhaps that would unclog whatever was blocking the fuel jets in the carburettor. With nothing else to do, her brain switched from panic to quiet, almost like her mind had detached itself from her body. She remembered a pilot friend saying he always took a loaded revolver to shoot at circling sharks. Jean shuddered. She didn't want to die that way. Instead, she hoped the impact would kill her outright.

Jean had crashed many times before. She figured she must have used up her nine cat lives. There was no avoiding this one. And no one to rescue her. No caravan of Arabs would appear to help her, like they did on another flight. It was just her, the plane and the deep, deep sea. Nobody would ever know what happened to her. Newspapers would say she'd disappeared over the ocean like so many other pilots.

Five minutes from impact Jean prayed. With her eyes glued to the unwinding altimeter, she asked the gods to intervene. 'Help me!'

Jean looked at the calm sea below her. No, she wasn't ready to give up yet. She'd try to land the plane in the water and float as long as possible. Maybe someone would see her from the air or from a ship. Kicking off her shoes, she undid the buttons on her flying suit. Then, just before impact, she opened and closed the throttle lever again. Nothing changed. This was it.

With her taut nerves bristling with adrenalin, Jean prepared to land. Suddenly, the engine roared like a clap of thunder and burst into life. The Gypsy Moth skimmed the surface of the sea. Jean thrust the throttle lever to its limit, and the plane rose. She held her breath until it reached a safe cruising height. She'd made it!

Her heart hadn't stopped beating wildly when the engine spluttered again. The plane dipped. Not again! She pumped the throttle. But this time, it kick-started straight away.

For the next three hours, the engine coughed and spluttered continuously. Jean dragged her eyes

away from the altimeter and compass to look at the concertina of map cards, guiding the plane towards Timor. On landing, Jean offered thanks to the gods. In the hangar, a Dutch mechanic leaned over the engine. 'Yah, that Australian dust must have caused a temporary blockage in the fuel system.'

Jean nodded. There was only one way to solve that. She cleaned the fuel filter and the carburettor jets and filled the fuel tank.

In the air, the plane kept misfiring, cutting out, before revving and coming back to life. That wasn't her only problem, though.

Jean avoided one storm. But, while flying across India and the Middle East, strong prevailing westerly headwinds buffeted the plane like a feather. She rocked side to side in the cockpit as the wind badgered the small plane. Jean looked at the map. She'd never beat her record.

Just as she flew over the Mediterranean Sea, the engine coughed and misfired even worse than before. Seeing the Italian Alps ahead, Jean pushed the throttle lever forward to climb, but the Moth refused to ascend. She'd hit the mountain if she didn't turn back. Jean spun the plane around, the engine firing only intermittently, and semi-glided down and then carried on to Marseilles in France. She might still have time to break her record. But luck was not with her.

After climbing out of the cockpit, she noticed the plane had a flat tyre. She threw her hands into the air. There was no way she was going to beat that record now. Jean locked herself in a room at the aerodrome and refused to talk to anyone.

While flying over France the next day, the engine cut out. It picked up seconds before she had to make a forced landing in a soggy field. Jean arrived back in England seventeen days and sixteen hours after leaving Darwin, two and a half days longer than her last flight. But she was the first female to do a return trip.

Not long after her return, she bought a new Percival Gull airplane and broke the world record for women and men flying from England to Brazil. In 1936, Jean flew from England to New Zealand, the first person to fly the whole route. On the way back, she broke the record between Australia and England again. Jean was the first person to hold the England to Australia solo record in both directions. After that, World War II intervened, and she never flew again.

SIR EDMUND HILLARY – A PERILOUS TRACTOR RIDE TO THE SOUTH POLE

Scott Base to Shackleton Base, Antarctica, 14 October 1957 to 4 January 1958

After Sir Edmund Hillary and Tenzing Norgay climbed Mt Everest, the highest mountain in the world, Edmund went in search of more adventures. When British scientist Dr Vivian Fuchs asked Edmund to set up supplies across Antarctica to enable a British team to traverse the continent, Edmund readily agreed. But he had a contingency plan . . .

Needle-like icy wind whipped Edmund's face as he drove the first modified Massey Ferguson tractor out of Scott Base on 14 October 1957. His team drove two tractors, a Weasel snowmobile and towed a caboose (a caravan on skis) and sledges.

The sun's red orb dressed the surrounding mountains in purple robes, taking Edmund's mind off the freezing temperatures and his aching backside from sitting on an uncomfortable metal seat for long hours. He tensed his muscles, constantly looking for crevasses. At the foot of a glacier, he sighted a black dot in the distance. It soon morphed into tents, two dog teams and stacks of stores, waiting for them at Skelton Depot.

Two days later, the dog teams raced ahead of them, as they passed through glaciers, a trough and up snowy slopes. Fifty knot gusty winds battered them as they neared the plateau, with the temperature dropping to minus 36 degrees Celsius. Edmund struggled to see 10 metres in front of him in the white-out conditions. He walked bent double in front of the tractors, following the dogs' footprints in the snow, checking for cracks and snow bridges in the ice.

One evening, Edmund received a telegram urging them to wait at Depot 700 for Dr Fuchs's party; he'd been delayed several weeks. 'That's the last thing I wanted to do,' Edmund later recalled. They'd miss their ship back home if they stayed too long. They had to leave the Antarctic soon or else they'd be stuck there for another winter. Injuries, illness and malfunctioning equipment forced his decision. Edmund sent a message back. 'We are heading hell-bent for the Pole, God willing and crevasses permitting,'. It would mean he'd be the first to reach it, after British explorer Robert Scott's disastrous attempt in 1912.

Edmund's body ached and his head throbbed with a temperature, as he pressed on through the gale-force winds. Each day they covered 12 to 55 kilometres, depending on the terrain. On the worst days, Edmund stood up in his tractor, steering with one hand over hummocks and through hollows.

The hummocks and hollows continued to increase in size and regularity. Edmund drove at full speed to warn the lead tractor. But before he could catch up, the party halted.

'An unpleasant sight met my eyes. The lead tractor was now on firm ground, but behind it was a great open hole – so big that it was hard to see how the tractor had managed to get clear of it,' he wrote in his diary

The second tractor hadn't been so lucky. It lay at a sharp angle with one of its snow-wheels dangling in the crevasse. Edmund prodded the ground around the lead tractor with his ice axe and found they were on thin ice; crevasses sliced through the ground. He marked out a route and with his nerves on edge he inched the tractor over the snow bridges, expecting them to crumble at any moment. After he parked it on safe ground, he let out his breath. They dragged the sledges to safety, but their constant driving over the same track had opened more crevasses.

They tied the three vehicles together and attached them to the trapped tractor. Edmund gave the signal, released the clutch on the snowmobile and jerked forward, the tracks skidding in the snow. *We're not going to do it!* Then he shot forward like a

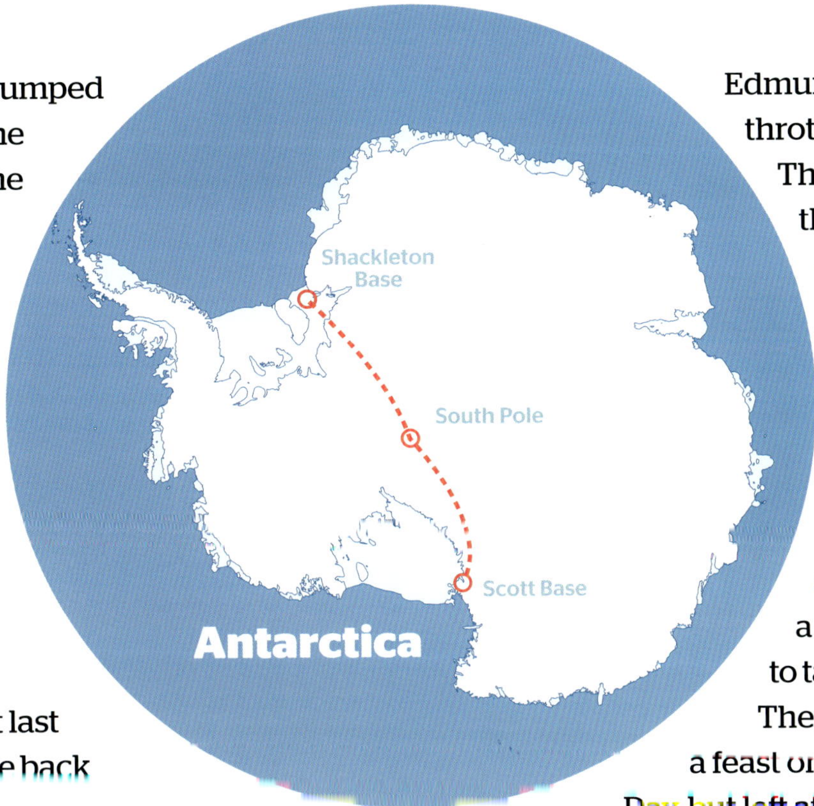

cork out of a bottle. Edmund jumped off the snowmobile to see if the tractor had made it out or if the rope had torn. He heaved a sigh of relief when he saw the last tractor had broken free. But when he looked behind it, he gasped. The crevasse had quadrupled in size. He crept to the edge. Sheer ice walls dropped to fathomless depths, enough to house a hundred tractors. They clapped each other on the back, but Ed's smile didn't last long – he now had to navigate back through this risky landscape.

Edmund drove the lead tractor, with the others roped behind him. When he stopped to see if the other men had also got through, he found the last tractor had punched a hole through a snow bridge. He held his breath to see if it would fall through, but then it lurched forward as the other vehicles pulled it to safe ground. A while later, Edmund's tractor inched across another snow bridge.

'My nerves were tense with expectation as I clattered onto the near side and then into the centre.'

He thought he'd made it when suddenly there was a thud beneath him, and his tractor tipped backwards. Edmund grabbed onto the sides to prevent himself falling into the crevasse. The bridge had gone.

'For a few awful moments we teetered on the lip of the crevasse, with the tracks clawing at the edge and the nose high in the air.'

Edmund revved the throttle some more. The tractor edged up the steep wall of the crevasse and then thumped onto the far side.

'Somewhat shaken I turned off the motor and scrambled out for a look. The hole was a beauty, big enough to take the tractor.'

They stopped for a feast on Christmas Day, but left at 7 pm, eager to reach the finish line. They travelled all night, with the sun shining all twenty-four hours. The soft snow made it slow progress. Edmund worried whether he was steering the crew in the right direction and if they'd have enough fuel. Exhausted, they stopped when Edmund spied a black dot in the distance. He peered through his binoculars and saw a line of flags. At 12.30 pm on 4 January 1958, they drove into the South Pole Station. Edmund climbed out of his tractor seat for the last time and clapped the backs of his fellow travellers. They'd made it!

Sir Edmund Hillary waited at the Pole for Dr Fuchs's team, who arrived sixteen days later. Ed helped the British party complete their trek to Scott Base, and then sailed to New Zealand, arriving on 17 March 1958 to a hearty welcome.

PAUL CAFFYN – KAYAKING AROUND AUSTRALIA IN 360 DAYS

Circumnavigation of Australia's coastline, 28 December 1981 to 23 December 1982

To say Paul Caffyn enjoyed the challenge of long-distance kayaking is an understatement. He'd already circumnavigated New Zealand and the United Kingdom, before taking on the first-ever journey around Australia's coast. After fourteen months of planning and training, he put on his wetsuit and spray skirt and launched his kayak from Queenscliff near Melbourne on 28 December 1981. Over three months, he paddled up the east coast, encountering curious sharks and rays, as well as deadly jellyfish. But he was yet to meet his biggest challenge.

Paul left Port Douglas and waved goodbye to his ground crew. He wouldn't see them for another month, as they couldn't get access to the coast around northern Queensland. He'd miss their support and friendship. Sometimes that was all that stood between him and giving up this mad idea of circumnavigating Australia.

A fresh easterly breeze chased Paul as he paddled over the bouncy chop through Owen Channel to a sandy beach. He turned on the radio for a weather update. The forecaster warned of two tropical cyclones, one heading south of Townsville and the second near the Gulf of Carpentaria. *Too far away for him to worry about, he thought.*

On Wharton Reef, he climbed a steel ladder to the top of a light tower to get a view of his next destination. The wind whistled and whined, and whitecaps rode on rough seas. Should he camp nearby instead of battling onwards? *Will I even see Stainer Islet in this murky weather?* It was a tiny island in the far northern Great Barrier Reef, hard enough to find on a fine day.

He pushed on, constantly checking his compass to see if he was heading in the right direction. Drizzling rain reduced visibility even more. Three hours later, he still hadn't spotted the small island. Had he missed it? He ran through his options. *Should I detour west or tackle a 32-kilometre run for the mainland shore?* Just then, he saw an isolated fang of exposed coral. He hoped it was Iris Reef joining Stainer Islet. He turned and paddled around it, punching through the breaking surf, avoiding patches of reef.

Torrential rain drenched him as he pulled the bow out onto the coral sand. To warm himself, he ran around the triangular-shaped sandbank, finding vines and grasses in the centre and one lone stunted Australian pine tree. Above the high-water mark, a mob of teenage pelicans nestled on the beach. Paul pitched his tent nearby.

The next day, violent squalls buffeted his tent. To stop it from being blown away, he pegged it to nearby driftwood. The sea was breaking over the edge of the island only 9 metres from his tent.

For the next two days, he stayed inside. The wind punched the walls and snatched at the corners. With nothing to do, Paul counted his food supplies and found he had only three days of meals left. His next food drop from his ground crew was two days away. He couldn't stay any longer or he'd run out of food. Paul dragged his kayak to the water's edge. Sand and grit smacked his face and raked through his hair and beard. Whenever he made a dash back to grab the rest of his stuff, the wind blew the boat towards the sea. Paul sprinted back in time to grab it. He waited until there was a lull, snatched his gear, and crammed it into his kayak. Then he crouched ready to push his kayak further out. But it was too difficult to hold onto his boat in the 3-metre waves. The sea was too rough. He had to drag his kayak and gear back up to the high-water mark.

All day Paul watched the fast-moving clouds. *Something nasty is brewing.* He turned on his radio, but it produced only static noise. It wasn't until he was eating his dinner that night that he could get reception. A clammy chill ran through his body when the broadcaster announced there was a cyclone warning, with destructive winds reaching

210 kilometres per hour, heading straight for him.

Paul packed his gear in case he had to move that night. He wished he had tried to make a run for one of the larger islands. A storm surge from the cyclone would completely cover the island.

Throughout the night, Paul listened to the cyclone warnings. If it came too close and swamped the island, he'd have to launch the kayak and ride the wild wind and seas until he reached the mainland. He could well die in the attempt.

At first light, he stepped outside his tent and had difficulty standing upright. The next broadcast told him one cyclone was only 50 kilometres north, and another was closing in southward.

Paul moved his tent to the centre of the island and tied everything to the scraggly tree, though he doubted it'd stay upright in cyclonic winds. At high tide, waves lapped over Paul's feet where he'd originally pitched his tent. To calm himself, Paul pictured himself playing a violin, an escape from the stark reality of the cyclone and his dwindling food supplies.

With head down, leaning into the wind, he walked around the islet. Four brown coconuts nestled in washed-up flotsam. He smacked one open and guzzled the fresh milk. At the low-tide mark, he found a clump of oysters growing on the remains of an old steel navigation beacon. He cooked up the coconut meat and oysters for dinner.

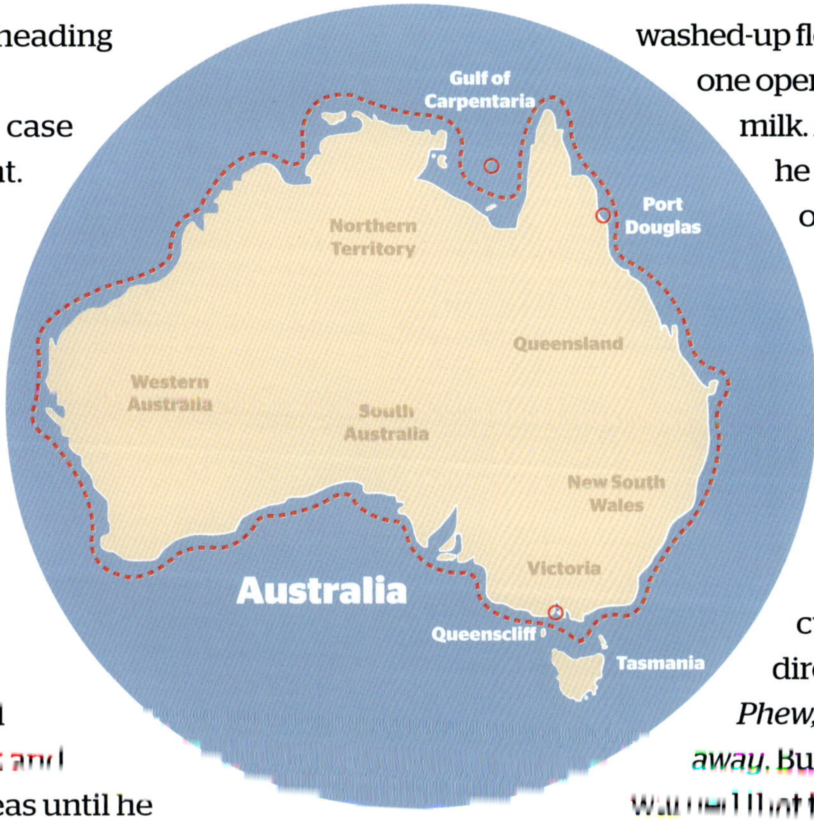

The weather forecaster announced later that day that one cyclone had changed direction towards Cairns. *Phew, it was much further away*. But then the speaker warned that there was a new tropical low forming right near Paul!

The next morning while eating breakfast, he heard there was a wind warning in place. But when Paul looked up at the scudding clouds, he saw patches of blue sky. He packed his gear into the kayak, ready to take a chance if the wind eased.

This time, Paul took the risk. He headed for the mainland, prepared to pull up on any island bigger than the last one he'd been stranded on. The wind eased later that morning and he made his destination. Paul continued his journey around the 15,000-kilometre coastline of Australia. It would take him 360 days. He would have a few more scares, but this terrifying experience had shown him he had the resilience and common sense to get through them.

MATAHI BRIGHTWELL – TAHITI TO NEW ZEALAND IN A WAKA

Tahiti–Cook Islands–Hicks Bay, New Zealand, 28 October 1985 to 31 December 1985

A chance encounter between Francis Cowan, a traditional Tahitian navigator, and New Zealand master carver Matahi Brightwell began an exciting project. They started making an ocean-going waka in New Zealand and finished it in Tahiti. After trialling the double-hulled waka, named *Hawaiki-nui*, they intended sailing back to New Zealand using traditional navigational methods. They would have no modern devices or maps to help them. Their goal: to prove that Polynesians had travelled to Aotearoa in waka. But they didn't get off to a great start.

Twice they left harbours, waving goodbye to their well-wishers, only to sit for hours waiting for the wind to blow in. Matahi was so fed up in Moorea, their first stop, that he turned to Francis.

'If the wind doesn't pick up soon, I'm swimming back to the harbour.'

Francis pointed to the far distance. 'The wind from the mountains will come down and push us out of the shelter of the island between 1 and 2 am.'

And it did!

It was a lesson for Matahi that he was travelling with a master navigator. Francis could read the wind, the stars and the currents. Matahi just had to trust and learn from him. The winds soon picked up to 30 knots, and the waka took off like a rocket – so fast they struggled to gain control of the bucking craft. Matahi crawled around the deck, not willing to risk standing up and being thrown off the waka.

Francis warned the crew they needed to wear a harness at all times. 'If you fall off, we can't turn around and pick you up.'

The sailors took turns being on watch. On the six-hour watches, Francis and Englishman Alex Roper navigated. Matahi, Greg Cuthers from Mangaia in the Cook Islands, and Rodo Parau from the Austral Islands took turns steering, adjusting sails and fishing.

Matahi kept his eyes peeled for the waves that criss-crossed over two coral heads in the passage when they sailed into Uturoa Harbour on Ra'iatea Island. The successful passage increased Matahi's confidence in their boat and their sailing skills, after their becalmed beginning.

After fixing a few parts and stocking up their stores, they left five days later. A boat towed them out of the channel. As soon as they were free of the tow ropes, they hoisted their sails and headed towards the port of Mirimiri, the traditional departure point for Rarotonga.

Francis showed Matahi how the streamers on the mast helped them keep on course. If they changed angle, they were off course. When the streamers dipped that indicated the wind had dropped. They knew the wind was blowing strongly if the streamers were horizontal. If they pointed stiffly, it was time to reduce the sail area, so they didn't capsize. At night, they could still see the white streamers. But they could also check whether they were on target by realigning the waka with Planet Venus and the Southern Cross stars.

On the third day out of Ra'iatea, the streamers flicked upwards. The crew fastened everything down and reduced the sail. *Hawaiki-nui* rode the monstrous waves, while the men clutched onto the mast and their harnesses.

'The wind must be around 80 knots,' Francis shouted. The wind whipping away his words.

Matahi blanched. Their waka could capsize in these ferocious gale-force winds. One nasty squall blasted over the waka and cracked the mast. The next squall was too much, and the mast bent in two places, toppling into the water, along with the sails.

Francis called out to Alex. 'Throw out the sea anchor.' Then he ordered Matahi to bring in the steering paddles and rudder. 'We don't want those broken or lost in these huge seas.'

Francis supervised the rest of the crew hauling up the mainmast. His calmness helped Matahi quieten his feelings of panic. For the next thirty-six

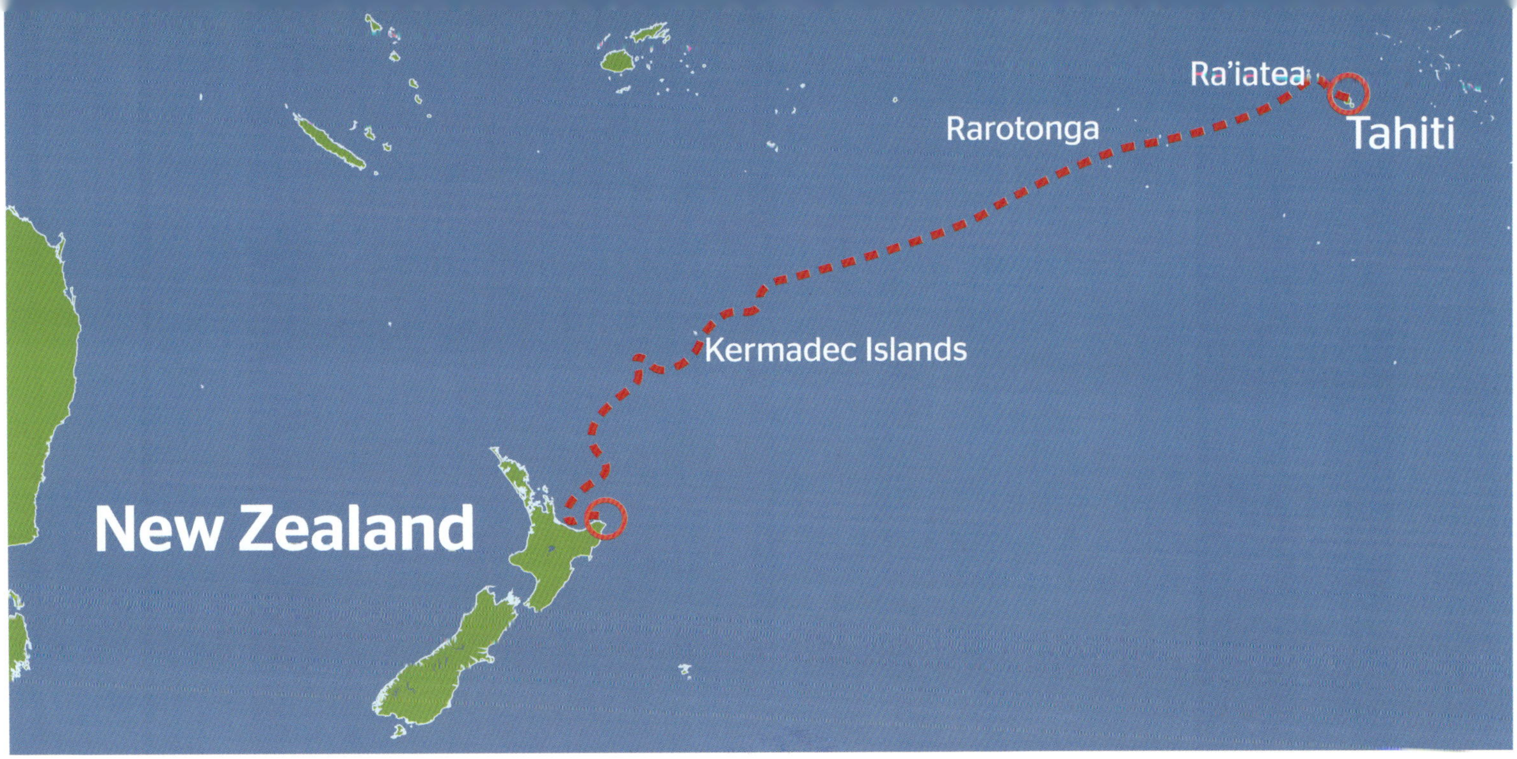

hours, the crew repaired the front stays that held up the mast and resurrected the shortened mast. Matahi worried that its lower height would slow them down. But it sailed as fast as it had before the accident. They limped into Rarotonga two days later than predicted.

A huge crowd greeted them as they ran *Hawaiki-nui* up onto the beach, in traditional Polynesian style. Over the next two weeks, they fixed their forward mainmast with replacement bamboo. They strengthened the mast with bamboo splints, refitted the boom and made sure that the lashings for the sails fitted the circumference of the new mast. In between the hard work, the locals invited the crew to feasts.

On 29 November, they left Ngatangiia for Aotearoa. The weather doused them in rain for most of the next twenty-two days. One day, Greg hooked a shark, but it was too heavy to heave on board. He jumped on its back and hacked off its head and guts to make it lighter. Matahi watched open-mouthed, as another shark ate the discarded head close by. Once Matahi got over the shock, he helped haul the shark onto the deck.

From then on, the blacktip sharks followed them for days on end. They snapped up any scraps they threw overboard. It made the men edgy, especially when they had to hang over the edge of the canoe to go to the toilet. Matahi had visions of a shark biting his bare backside. To get rid of one school, they stopped sailing and made sure not to throw any scraps into the sea. After a while, the sharks got the message – no more easy food for them – and swam off.

Francis ordered the sails down hoping the wind would change. After four days of drifting with the currents it hadn't. They had no choice but to sail through the middle of the Kermadec Reef. They stayed up all night to navigate past the rocks and reefs. **A pod of whales and then an albatross escorted them closer to the North Island. But then they had to go further offshore when not one but two storms head-butted them. Rescue services sent out a fishing trawler to help tow them into Hicks Bay in the East Cape region on New Year's Eve, 1985, where thousands of people greeted them. They had provided proof of traditional voyaging from the Pacific Islands.**

HELEN THAYER – FIRST WOMAN TO TRAVERSE SOLO TO THE MAGNETIC NORTH POLE

Little Cornwallis Island–Magnetic North Pole–Helena Island, Canada, 30 March 1988 to 25 April 1988

Months before Helen Thayer left on her solo trek to the Magnetic North Pole, she ran, hiked, skied and kayaked to build up her strength. She also planned for every worst-case scenario. Helen starved herself before and after treks, so she'd be mentally prepared if it should happen. She tested her gear in an Arctic environment to make sure it would keep her warm in freezing temperatures. She spent two weeks with Inuit hunters learning how to survive ice packs and polar bears, the Arctic's top predator. When the Inuit couldn't dissuade her from going on the dangerous trip, they insisted she take a part-husky part-wolf dog. She named him Charlie, and they spent a couple of days getting to know each other. Now, she was finally ready to take the first steps . . .

On a crisp, sunny morning in minus 43 degrees Celsius, Helen hauled her loaded sled from the frozen ground of Little Cornwallis Island onto Crozier Strait sea ice. Just before she left, an Inuit hunter warned her a polar bear was nearby. He tried to persuade her to delay her trip. But she was keen to get started and figured she might as well meet her greatest fear sooner rather than later. Besides, she had her trusty Charlie beside her, dragging his own sled.

Helen tugged her sled through gaps in 3-metre-high pinnacles. Soon she had an eerie feeling she was being watched. Helen swivelled her head around, watching for movement. She told Charlie, 'I'm depending on you to warn me if a bear comes our way.' Her heart pumped high-speed every time they crossed fresh bear tracks.

While setting up her tent that evening, the wind chill reached minus 73 degrees Celsius. She put on insulated mittens and windmilled her numb hands to pump blood into them. That first night she had a restless sleep, listening for sounds, worrying a polar bear might sneak up.

On her second day in the icy wilderness, Helen hadn't finished packing her sled when she heard Charlie growling and straining at his chain. About 200 metres away, a mother polar bear advanced towards them, with two cubs trailing behind. Helen grabbed her rifle and flare gun and sidled over to Charlie. She clipped the snarling husky to her sled, all the time keeping eye contact with the bear.

Helen fired a warning shot to the bear's left. The mother ignored the whip-like snap of the sonic boom. She kept approaching even after Helen shot two flares. On the third red flare, the mother glanced at her cubs, making sure they were safe, then ambled in a half circle towards Helen. Charlie snarled and snapped. Still, the mother advanced. Helen fired more shots and flares. When the mother was about 100 metres away, she stopped, turned north, and plodded away. *Phew, I'm not worth the risk.*

Twice more that day, she encountered polar bears. Her shot nerves and blistered hands made her doubt whether she should continue. There were plenty of reasons to give up. But when Helen considered how she had successfully driven off three polar bears, she convinced herself to carry on. Before going to bed, she hugged Charlie and thanked him for saving her life.

Over the next two days, she skied around pressure ridges, icy mounds and a 9-metre-high iceberg. Dry, sandy snow blew into her face, icing up her face mask, covering her eyelashes in icicles. Her tracks criss-crossed over polar bear and fox footprints. Charlie's ferocious barking shooed off another curious polar bear.

After skiing through Polar Bear Pass, she stopped for a rest beside a large hummock of ice. Charlie growled, his black fur bristling. Helen grabbed her rifle and flare gun and stood beside the snarling dog. Suddenly an enormous bear appeared from behind the hummock and raced towards them. He flicked aside her sled with his massive paw. The bear stood on its hind legs and charged at them. Helen released Charlie's collar. He dashed towards the bear. Helen raised the rifle ready to shoot point blank. Just as she fired, the bear dropped on all fours. The bullet whistled over its head. Charlie hung onto the bear's hind leg. The bear twisted around, its teeth bared, trying to bite Charlie. They circled each other until the bear tore itself off and charged away with Charlie at his heels.

Her heart thumping, hands shaking, Helen stood waiting for Charlie to return. She worried he'd get lost or hurt. Minutes later, a black spot appeared. She prayed it was Charlie. He leapt in bounds towards her. Helen dropped her gun and ran towards him. They tumbled together in a warm hug.

For several days, an Arctic storm forced them to stay in the tent. Snow piled on the sides, threatening to topple the tent. A loud crack jolted Helen outside. *Was it a bear?* A white-out prevented her from seeing anything. Then it cracked again, and she saw the ice split open around her.

The next day, they had to step over many cracks in the ice. Sometimes it shortened or lengthened in front of their eyes. Charlie followed Helen's leaps over the cracked ice. She shuddered at the thought of falling into the ice-cold, ink black water between the fissures.

Five days later, Helen rounded King Christian Island. Ahead, black clouds threatened. Quickly, the storm bore down on her. She fastened everything to the ice. Suddenly, a sound like a jet engine blasted towards her. The wind ploughed into her body, lifting her off her feet and slamming her down onto the ice. She crawled closer to the sled, yanking the zipper shut to prevent more gear from being ripped out.

When the hellish wind died down, Helen

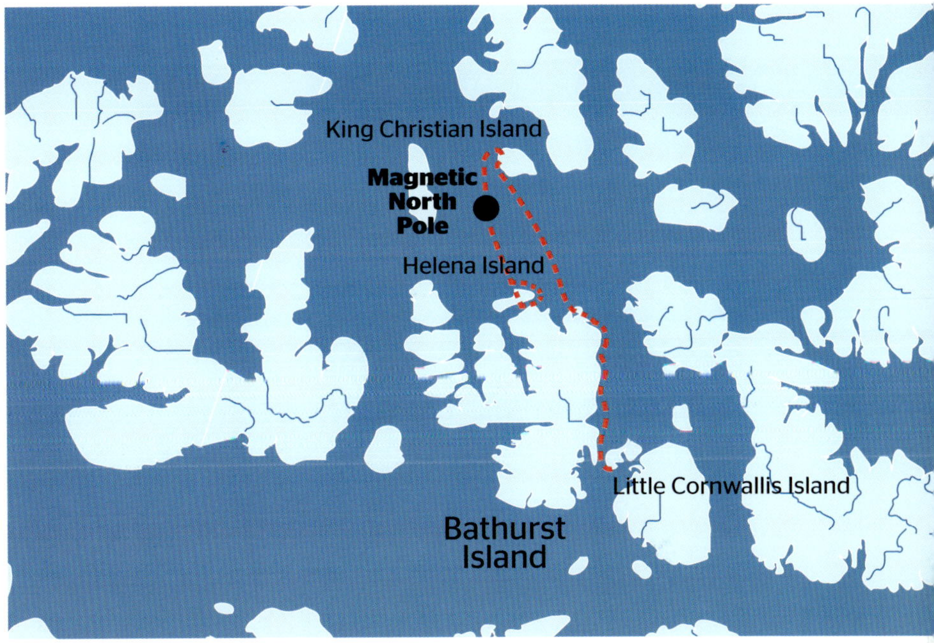

inspected her sled bag. All her food, most of the fuel, the spare stove and clothes had gone. Some packs of dog food from Charlie's sled had also blown away.

For the next eight days, Helen fed Charlie half-rations. He was used to starvation from his Inuit days. All she had left were five handfuls of walnuts. She melted ice for her day's ration of half a litre of water.

Helen and Charlie reached the Magnetic North Pole on day twenty-one. She was the first woman to do so on a solo expedition. Seven days later, through howling winds, crippling hunger and thirst, a swollen eye and blistered hands, she reached Helena Island. She called a plane on her radio and waited. Helen took Charlie home with her to Washington State, USA, where he quickly made friends with Helen's husband Bill and their three family dogs. Charlie would later join her on another journey into the Arctic world.

LYDIA BRADEY – FIRST WOMAN TO CLIMB MT EVEREST WITHOUT OXYGEN

Everest Base Camp to Mt Everest summit, 13 October to 16 October 1988

Lydia Bradey dreaded sport at school. So much so, she'd vomit on sports day. Her mother enrolled her in a mountain craft course at fourteen years old to give her confidence. She loved it. Three years later, she climbed Mt Aspiring and at eighteen years old, Aoraki/Mt Cook. From then on, she aspired to climb the highest mountains in the world. To prepare herself, Lydia spent nine months in Yosemite Valley, California, rock-climbing the ten 'Big Walls'. For seven of those climbs, she was the first female to ascend. She was also the first woman from the Southern Hemisphere to climb Gasherbrum II (8035 metres) in the Kashmir region without assisted oxygen. Now she was ready to climb the highest mountain in the world: Everest (8850 metres), without assisted oxygen. She'd be the first woman ever to do it. *If she survived.*

Lydia pulled herself up the 700-metre vertical height on fixed ropes left by other climbers. The wind buffeted her every step as she climbed onto the Lhotse Face, then dropped to camp four called the South Col. On the flat ice shelf, several tents bent into the wind. She waved hello to a team of Spanish climbers and two Sherpa guides.

Inside a tent, she found a French climber huddled in his sleeping bag, breathing through his oxygen mask. She nodded, dropped her pack, and started her routine of melting ice and drinking it, eating a muesli bar, and then resting. At 2 am, Lydia followed the Frenchman and his two guides, as well as the Spanish team, up a rock-scattered slope leading to a shelf called the Balcony. With no moon to illuminate her pathway, she followed her head torch light, memorising landmarks. She needed to know those coming back. Any wrong move and she could fall into a crevasse or slide down a slope. Soon, the French and Spanish teams were dots of lights in front of her. Without an oxygen tank to assist her breathing, Lydia travelled much slower.

Up ahead, the Spanish team stopped and huddled around a lump. Their raised voices drifted down with the wind. Then they continued up the slope. When the Frenchman and his guides reached the same lump, they too stopped. They waved their hands about as they talked. But instead of moving up, they turned and came back down.

'Expedition over!' the Frenchman said as he passed her, continuing downwards.

She quickened her step, eager to see why. When she came to the lump, she looked down. A Sherpa guide lay face down in the snow. She stared at his bare feet, his hiking boots gone. But there was nothing she could do. The Frenchman and his guides raced to fetch help.

Lydia carried on up a steep slope, her boots crunching in the crusty snow. She chipped the packed ice with her axe, counting every step to help motivate her. As the sun lightened the sky, she stopped to catch her breath. She lifted her drink bottle to sip its contents. The frozen water thunked against her mouth, not a drop wetting her lips. *How dumb of me. I should have brought a thermos like some of the other climbers*. Lydia frowned. *Will I be okay without that extra litre of water?* She'd have to risk it.

To ensure her safety, Lydia did her flight checks. She patted her head. Hat on. Adjusted her goggles. Pulled up her mittens, and scuffed the crampons on her boots. Check. Everything working. She was ready. But in the pit of her stomach, she felt so alone. The silence was deafening.

At the South Summit, the Spanish team met her on their downward track. They'd already reached the summit and returned, taking two hours. *I'm too slow*.

A Spanish climber asked, 'Will you keep going?'

If she did, she'd be on her own. It was getting late. Should she return with them? Then her resolve kicked in. 'I'm going up.'

'You'll die,' he answered.

Her eyes widened. Would she? She watched them shuffle past. *Shuffle?* She looked closer. They had tied themselves to short ropes to help a member who was suffering altitude sickness. *No wonder they think I'll die. He had an oxygen mask. I don't.*

The sun shone on Everest's peak, bathing it in golden light. The goal visible. In reach. Lydia squared her shoulders. *I can do this*. But a shiver of fear ran through her. She tramped up a series of dips and rises towards a flat shelf called the Hillary Step. Ahead, a crevasse blocked her way. She sunk to her knees and crawled over a snow bridge to even out her weight. On the other side, she slumped onto her backside. Glancing back, she saw the last member of the Spanish team watching her. He waved and descended out of sight. Now she was truly alone.

Her nerves caught in her throat. She knew she had enough energy to reach the summit, but would she have enough to descend? She'd never know if she didn't push on. She had to have faith in herself.

On the Hillary Step, a rope blew in the wind. She grabbed it, feet on either side, using it to steady herself. She edged onto a ledge, up to a knob, not daring to look down. An overwhelming feeling of tiredness and breathlessness slowed her down. The icy wind buffeted her as she climbed up, scrambled onto the summit, and collapsed onto the flat surface. *I did it!*

The wind tossed her as she gazed at the orange light glowing along the horizon. Pink wispy clouds drifted past, and puffs of snow rolled over the Tibetan Plains. *I'm on top of the world!*

After ten minutes, she stood up, feeling completely shattered. But she couldn't stay any longer. The thought of not finding her tent in the dark terrified her. Lydia automatically did her flight checks and climbed down. Time and time again, she had to force herself to keep going.

In the waning light, Lydia caught up with the Spanish team.

'How did you go?' one asked.

'I made the summit!'

The Sherpa guide patted her shoulder. 'Strong girl!'

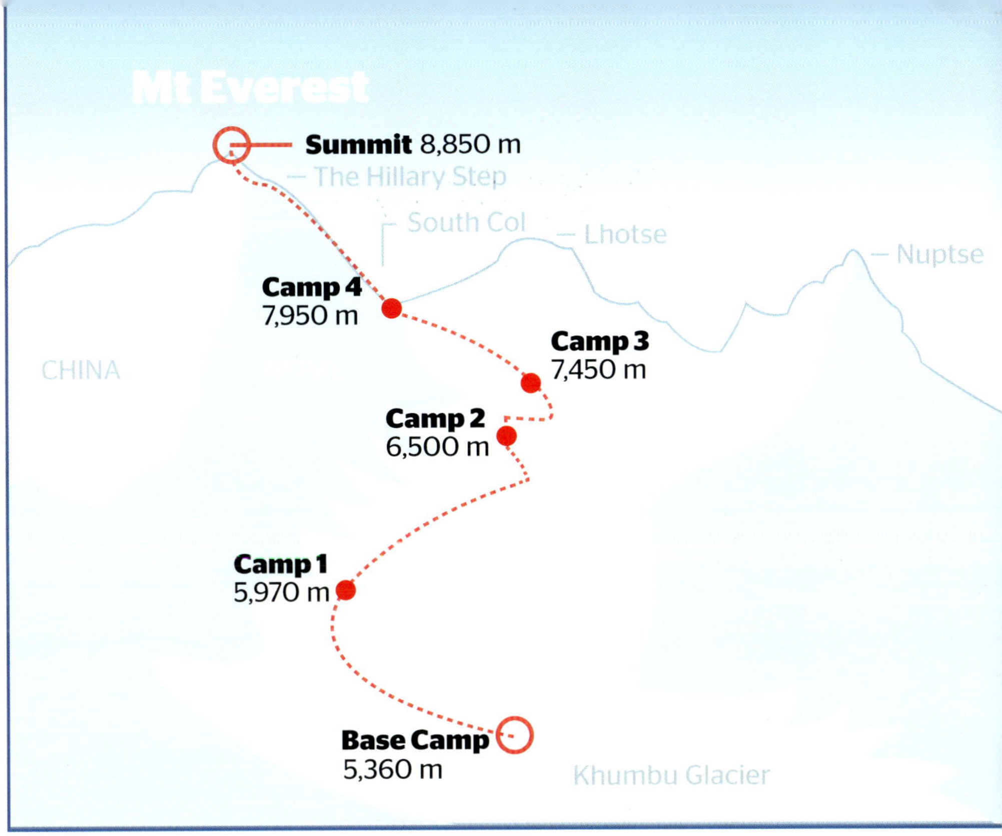

The next day, Lydia stayed in her tent until midday, recuperating from the exhaustion, before returning to Base Camp on 16 October 1988. Years later, Lydia climbed Everest from the south (Nepal) and the north (Tibet) six times. She was also the first woman to climb Dhaulagiri (8157 metres) in Nepal, and Broad Peak (8051 metres) in Pakistan. She became an International Mountain and Ski Guide in 2000 and has worked as an alpine guide in Nepal, Antarctica, Argentina, Kyrgyzstan and Mongolia.

LISA TAMATI – CROSSING A FORBIDDEN MILITARY ZONE IN THE WESTERN DESERT

Farafra to Bahariya Oasis, Western Desert, Egypt, 1 April 1997 to 8 April 1997

Lisa Tamati had just traversed the Sahara Desert in Tunisia, and the Arabian Desert in Egypt, when a friend invited her to walk through the Western Desert that bordered Egypt and Libya, a forbidden zone that was heavily guarded by Egyptian military. She had only two days to organise supplies in Cairo. Lisa threw out spare clothes to fit in 20 litres of water. Her 35-kilogram pack was now so heavy, fellow walkers had to lift it onto her back. Along with her team, Paul, Alvis and Gunther, she rode a bus to Farafra, the closest town to the military zone.

The foursome sat on the edge of the desert under a palm tree, waiting for nightfall. Three Egyptians dressed in white tunics sauntered up to them. *Was the game up before they'd even started?*

'What are you doing here?' the locals asked, suspicion pinched on their faces.

Alvis smiled. 'We're enjoying the view of the fortress ruins in the sunset.'

The Egyptians wandered off. Lisa blew out her breath, relieved. If the military caught them and searched their bags, they'd find satellite pictures of the area and an old GPS navigation system. With no accurate maps available, it was their only means of finding their way in the desert. The military would suspect them of being Libyan spies and jail them.

As soon as the sun disappeared, Alvis, the leader of the group, set a fast pace in the desert, using the GPS to navigate. If they became lost, no one would know where they were. Lisa shrugged off the fear they could die out there.

Lisa followed behind, stumbling in the deep sand. She could barely see her feet or the bumpy ridges made by military jeeps. *They must be close*. The possibility of being caught in the closed military zone sent a shiver through her.

They walked throughout the night to put as much distance between the military outpost and themselves as possible. At midnight, they stopped for a rest, but the cold quickly seeped into their bodies. They carried on to keep warm. At 6 am, the sun rose. Strange white mushroom-shaped formations and sand waves made from limestone extended to a range of mountains in the far distance. Her imagination picked out a sphinx, camels and human faces in the weathered sculptures.

The next morning sun's rays cast orange-pink hues over chalk towers that popped out of the ground like large anthills. Nearby, a spectacular canyon laid out its carpet of golden sand between its crumbling walls. It led them towards a flat-top mountain.

Lisa struggled up the slippery scree, her heavy pack bruising her hips. At the top, she dropped to her knees and let the backpack slide off. When she caught her breath, she saw an unending series of mountains and valleys. She groaned. They had to climb up and down each one to reach the other side. The scorching sun reached 42 degrees Celsius, but they continued. At midday, they collapsed under the shade of a rocky outcrop. When Lisa woke, the guys were comparing how much water they had left for the day. They were all drinking beyond their daily allowance. Not Lisa. She drank only one and a half bottles each night, figuring she'd sweat it out if she sipped it during the day.

Alvis calculated their mileage. 'We've only made 16 kilometres today.' They agreed they had to start earlier and walk longer, or they'd run out of water. Lisa cringed. Already she was struggling, but she didn't want to let the team down. But her back ached, her swollen feet were a mess and she was beyond thirsty. She said nothing. Lisa took stock of what she could change. Her pack was too heavy. She emptied the contents and threw half the food away, keeping the chocolates and dried fruit. Next, she tended to her blistered and bleeding feet. Then she stretched and trudged onwards.

Early morning, they reached the last mountain. Ahead was a vast sea of black volcanic sandhills. Her boots sunk deep into the slippery sand. It seeped into her shoes, chafing her raw feet. And there was no shade anywhere. The scorching sun burnt her skin, dried her swollen tongue and cracked her lips. Her throat was so dry she couldn't swallow water or eat anything even if she wanted to.

Twice, they thought they'd lost Gunther. Alvis found him disorientated, having given up hope of finding them.

That night, a sandstorm blew in. They rushed behind a sandhill and zipped up their sleeping bags. Lisa buried her head into its folds, like a caterpillar in a cocoon. Bucketsful of sand bashed their bodies. It sounded like heavy rain on a tin roof. Lisa feared being buried alive. At 3 am, the wind subsided. Lisa stood up. Sand dripped from her hair and clothes. It had gone up her nose, into her ears and crusted the outsides of her eyes.

Alvis set off, determined to make up time. Lisa had no time to drink her daily allowance. An hour into the fast pace, she felt woozy. Her eyes blurred and her legs trembled. Then everything went black. She woke up flat on her back like a helpless turtle, unable to right itself. The boys rushed to pick her up.

'Are you alright?' asked Alvis.

Lisa blinked her eyes. 'Yeah, don't know what happened.'

They continued, but five minutes later it happened again. They lifted her up again. She should have stopped and drunk water, but she was too proud to ask them to wait. On the third fall, she felt disorientated. After the fourth collapse, she walked dazed behind them. Finally, they reached the edge of a cliff and saw the Bawiti Depression before them.

When the black-powdered mounds started bouncing up and down and morphing into monsters, she realised she was hallucinating. Sensing something was wrong, Alvis took her hand and guided her down the steep cliff. She stumbled and followed blindly. When they reached the bottom, Lisa tore open her backpack and ripped out a bottle, glugging down the precious water. The liquid filled every dried-out cell in her body.

It was night-time when they approached Bahariya Oasis. They shook hands, congratulating each other. Then ducked down when they saw a guard holding a gun in a military lookout tower only 50 metres from them. They crept along the boundary until they found a hole and crawled through. They'd made it!

Once Lisa healed from the trip, she was thinking of her next endurance adventure. She'd compete in many ultramarathons throughout the hottest deserts in the world, as well as running from Cape Reinga to Bluff in Aotearoa.

CAM MCLEAY AND GARTH MACINTYRE – FINDING THE SOURCE OF THE NILE RIVER

Cairo, Egypt to Kigali, Rwanda, 20 September 2005 to 31 March 2006

Cam McLeay and Garth MacIntyre, along with their British friend Neil McGrigor, wanted to find the longest source of the Nile River. No one had before. They knew the trip wouldn't be easy. They might encounter aggressive rebels and deadly creatures such as crocodiles, hippos and lions, and in the rainforests, elephants. The explorers also needed to negotiate massive rapids while in searing heat. They thought they could handle anything . . .

Each day, Cam, Neil and Garth motored over 100 kilometres in their three inflatable boats, often weaving around heavily laden feluccas, traditional Nile craft. They waved to women and children washing their clothes, fishers laying their nets and men washing themselves in the Egyptian river. River police signalled them to slow down, but they didn't, heady with adventure fever.

Several times their inflatables hit sandbanks. The sudden stop propelled the driver and passenger into the murky disease-ridden waters. Once Cam caught a tuft of wind, near-somersaulted the boat and landed upright in the river. *Victory!*

At the Aswan Low and High Dams, a truck hauled their boats out and dropped them into Lake Nasser, the largest human-made lake in the world. That night they slept on their boat's Bimini top, watching the shooting stars streak across the sky, thrilled they were making their dream happen.

On the third day in Sudan, they crossed their first rapid. Nervously, they lashed their gear down, put on their lifejackets and helmets, and rode the white waters. It was a lot easier than they thought.

When they saw a large herd of cattle with cream hides and pointy horns resting on the riverbank, they slowed their boats for a closer look. Ghostly figures of naked boys coated in white ash and mud appeared. The nomadic Dinka tribespeople, some of the tallest people in the world, materialised around them. The herd-people brandished AK-47 rifles in farewell when they left.

Round the corner, foaming brown water thundered over and around boulders. With butterflies in their stomachs, they rode across the 3.2-kilometre stretch of rapids, dropped into a cauldron at the foot of the first torrent, and then zipped through a narrow gorge. *Phew! They couldn't believe they did it without capsizing.*

On 27 October, they followed the hyacinth flowers into Uganda. At Paraa, they carried their fuel bags to a depot. Two rotund hippos moved their hefty bottoms to allow Neil access to the pumps. One hippo followed them back to the river. They deflated their boats and flew them in their newly arrived microlight, an FIB – a flying inflatable boat. That night, they heard lions roaring across the river.

Back on the water, a large crocodile charged with its jaw open. Cam had no choice but to gun the motor and head straight for the reptile. At the last second, the crocodile ducked underwater, the outboard clipping the beast.

One afternoon, Neil misjudged how high he was flying. He tried to clear a treetop at the last minute. The FIB somersaulted into the vegetation. Cam and Garth charged through the trees, following the sound of the FIB crashing. They found it upside down and in pieces. Neil wobbled towards them, white with shock, and fell. Burn marks scorched his body, and his ankle looked broken.

Cam called a friend on the satellite phone. His friend agreed to help. But he needed coordinates so he could find them. Cam scouted the jungle, scaring off a baboon, and found an empty poachers' camp. At least, Cam hoped it had been poachers there. They didn't want to run into rebels. On Tuesday, 7 November, their friend Steve arrived. His soldiers carried the inflatables and gear past the rapids to their truck.

Steve drove the team and one soldier back to town. Suddenly, a man in ripped olive clothes stepped out of the grass. He raised a gun and fired at their vehicle. Bullets bounced off the engine and penetrated the driver's door. The car swerved. A stray bullet grazed Gareth's head. He pitched forward. The men hunched down, hearts pounding.

Their vehicle bounced and dropped into a gravel pit. The explorers kicked open the doors. Their guard disappeared into the elephant grass, taking his rifle with him. The rest bolted in different directions. Blood dripped from Garth's head as he hid behind a bush. He held his breath when feet padded towards him. Minutes ticked by. Then the animal moved off. When he thought it safe, he scrambled out. A lion's footprints were all that remained of the too-close visitor. Garth brushed a shaky hand through his hair and climbed a tree.

Neil hobbled only a short distance before his leg gave way. A rebel searched the grasses near him. Just before the rebel saw him, Neil stood up, hands raised. The rebel shoved a rifle at Neil's head. The two rebels signalled they wanted money, arms and clothes. Neil gave them what they wanted. They lit a bushel of grass and threw it into the car. Neil closed his eyes, thinking this was the end. Instead, he heard them run away with their haul. He opened his eyes and saw the flames flick across the seating. He doused the fire in the vehicle, then reached into the smouldering car for the radio and called for help.

Meanwhile, Cam had run barefoot towards Paraa. His cut feet ached and his lungs burned. He swung his head side to side every time he heard a rustle, snort or sigh. It could be a lion, elephant or hippo. He willed himself to keep going to raise the alarm. Then he heard a car coming towards him. *Was it the rebels?* He hid and watched it approach. Soldiers levelled guns at him. 'We've been looking for you,' the commander said. 'You are safe now.'

All survived except Steve the driver. The friends recovered at home, but they kept thinking about the unfinished journey. Four months later, they returned. Cam, Neil and Garth motored up the swollen Victoria Nile into Rwanda. Twenty days later, the river had dwindled to a creek. They left their inflatables behind and trekked through the jungle until the explorers found an ooze of water from a steep ridge. They had travelled over 6700 kilometres in three boats through five countries over 80 days and finally found the longest source of the Nile River!

LAURA DEKKER – YOUNGEST FEMALE TO SAIL SOLO AROUND THE WORLD

Portugal–Saint Martin–New Zealand, 4 August 2010 to 21 January 2012

Fourteen-year-old New Zealand-born Dutch citizen Laura Dekker yearned to sail around the globe by herself. She believed she had the skills to do it. But the Dutch authorities thought it too risky and took her to court eight times to stop her. When she passed her Dutch Boating exam, they refused to issue it. She didn't let that stop her. Laura and her father left the Netherlands in a 12-metre, two-masted ketch called *Guppy* on 4 August 2010 with his skipper ticket to Gibraltar. From there onwards, she was on her own. She sailed to the islands off the coast of Africa for several months, celebrating her fifteenth birthday and waiting for the hurricane season to end. On 19 December, she sailed into Saint Martin, a Caribbean Island, where she began her circumnavigation of the globe. She'd experience many challenges, but the ferocious storms in the Southern Hemisphere would be her biggest yet.

GUPPY

On 25 May 2011, after a tricky passage through dangerous reefs, Laura threw out the anchor into the muddy waters of Hiva Oa, one of the Marquesas Islands in the Pacific. The next morning, she hitched a ride to Customs and showed her papers. 'Have you honestly sailed here on your own?' asked the officer, disbelief written all over his face. She nodded. He stamped her documents while shaking his head.

For the next four months, Laura hopped from one Pacific island to the next. She wanted to stay longer on the tropical atolls with friendly locals, but a clock was ticking. She needed to cross the Indian Ocean to take advantage of the south-easterly trade winds and while she was at it, try to beat Australian Jessica Watson's world record of being the youngest person to sail the world solo.

After a stint in Darwin, fixing sails and celebrating her sixteenth birthday, she left its port.

Her next destination would be the longest yet – 6000 nautical miles (11,112 kilometres) to South Africa. For the next three weeks, she'd be completely on her own, and that's the way she liked it, just her and *Guppy* with the fresh wind on their faces … but that was not to be for the next fourteen days.

Flap, clunk, flap, clunk. Guppy's sails fluttered in the non-existent winds. Not enough to sail faster than two knots. She'd get nowhere at that speed. Laura turned on the motor. If she didn't, she'd drift back to Darwin.

On deck, Laura noticed a large wooden fishing vessel motoring straight for her. She raced below, calling the skipper on the radio to alert them. No one answered. If she didn't move, they'd crash. Laura altered her course and watched as the ship charged past with no one on lookout. Two hours later, it happened again. She wrote in her diary: 'A good thing I'm more alert than they are!'

The ghostly fishing boats unnerved her. She turned off her tracker so that no one would know where she was. Piracy was a real problem in this area, and on the radio, she heard there was a pirate attack near Madagascar. But she had promised her dad she'd text him twice a day to let him know her location.

On day sixteen, she finally felt wind. She wrote in her diary:

'… once the squalls have disappeared on the horizon I feel it – WIND! Wonderful wind. Guppy flies forward and is making real speed for the first time since Darwin. It's going well and she's jumping over the waves at a speed of 7 knots like a young foal, and looks as though she's enjoying it as much as her skipper.'

The waves became friskier, steeper and higher. *Guppy* rolled dangerously from side to side as she surfed the white foam. Laura thought about reducing the sail when a huge breaker crashed over *Guppy*, causing the boat to land on its side at the bottom of a trough. Water whooshed into the cockpit as she hung horizontally to the companionway. Once *Guppy* righted herself, Laura waited for the right moment to venture on deck. She waded through knee-deep water in the cockpit and attached her safety line to the rail to reef in the sails. Water flew over her, as she gathered in rope trailing in the water. Soaking wet, she sheltered below deck, while the breakers gathered height, then crashed over *Guppy* with force.

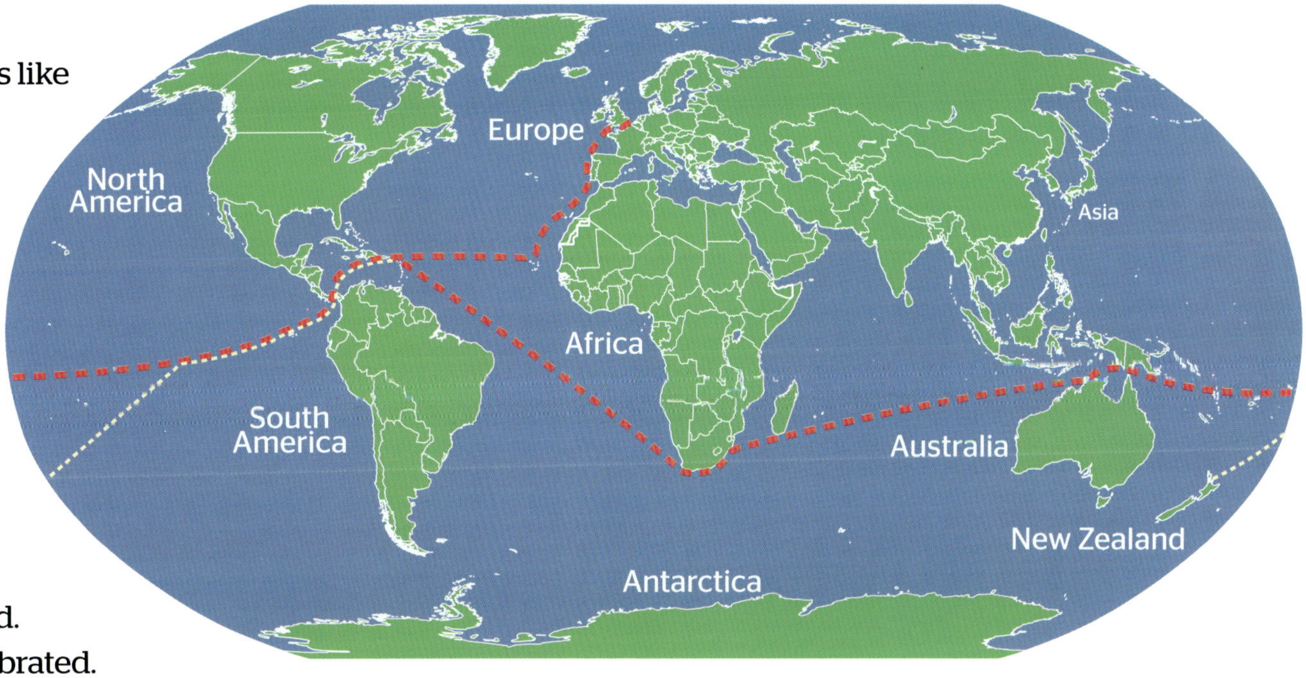

The yacht rode the waves like a rollercoaster.

But she was yet to face her worst storm. When sailing around the Cape of Good Hope, the weather forecast was for 35 knot winds, but they were more like 55 knots. Laura reduced her sails to slow the boat down from 12 knots – the fastest she'd ever travelled. Too fast for *Guppy*. She vibrated. The towering waves forced *Guppy* to twist sideways and fall flat in the trough. Wham! A massive breaker submerged the boat under a mass of foaming water. Everything flew around the cabin while *Guppy* righted herself. With a hammering heart, Laura brushed sea water and tangled hair off her face and reduced sail even more.

Around dawn, the gusts of wind had increased to 65 knots. Through the dim light, she saw a mountain range. A weak 'Guppy, Guppy,' called on the VHF, and Laura replied.

'I'm standing on top of Table Mountain, and we think we can see you from time to time,' her father said.

'You could be right, Dad. *Gup* is spending more time underwater than above it –' Bang!

'What's happening?'

'Oh, nothing, Guppy almost got flattened by a wave . . .'

Laura loved hearing his voice, but she had to get back outside and unfurl the sail so she could head into port. She was shaking with cold by the time she dropped anchor in Cape Town, South Africa.

On 12 December, Laura set sail for Saint Martin with no stops. She threw on a party hat, lit up the little Christmas tree she'd been given in Cape Town, and floated streamers across the bunks on Christmas Day. On New Year's Eve, she celebrated with music and glow-sticks. Throughout the long trip, squalls battered her boat, seabirds left their calling cards all over the deck, and flying fish landed in her cabin. Forty days later, Laura arrived back in Saint Martin, 366 days after she had left it to travel solo around the globe. A flotilla of boats accompanied *Guppy* into port. Laura hugged her family and gave media interviews, but she stayed only a week in the limelight before sailing on her own to her birth country, New Zealand. Her message to everyone who had followed her voyage: 'Follow your dreams!'

MARK WATSON AND HANA BLACK – CYCLING THE AMERICAS

Deadhorse, Alaska to Coyhaique, Chile, 6 June 2016 to March 2020

For four years, long-distance cyclists Hana Black and Mark Watson pedalled through sixteen countries over 46,000 kilometres following the American Cordillera, the mountainous spine that stretches over two vast continents. Mark and Hana were no strangers to such an epic journey, having already cycled throughout New Zealand, the Philippines, China, and South East Asia. Physically and psychologically, they were ready to bike off the beaten tracks. They knew they would encounter many challenges such as deserts, jungles, mountain passes and extreme weather, and they might encounter bears and mountain lions. But they had an attitude that they'd take each day as it came.

On a freezing day, Mark and Hana pedalled their bikes out of the oil-mining town of Deadhorse. They carried bear spray and bear bells at the ready in case they ran into trouble.

They cycled on unsealed highways through vast landscapes of Arctic tundra and forest, passing moose in shallow lakes. Thunderstorms threatened, hail pelted them and ice nibbled at their fingers.

Each day, they rose before dawn, ate breakfast in their tent, packed up camp and rode for five to eight hours, stopping for breaks. They continued until dusk, then pitched their tent beside spruce-lined lakes, watching beavers building their lodges. In Canada, they passed glaciers, avalanche debris, a fiord and a canal. Logs strapped together floated downriver. First Nation totem poles dotted the roadside.

In British Columbia, a black bear crossed the road, stopping to eat berries on the verge. Hana and Mark waited for it to disappear into the bush, bear spray clutched in their hands. But it wasn't afraid of them or the passing cars. A truck driver wound down his window. 'I'll drive slowly past. Why don't you ride beside me, out of sight of the bear?' They did, wary of it picking up their scent as they cycled past.

Another time, Mark cycled ahead, looking for a grassy verge to camp in the dusky light. Behind, Hana shouted a warning. He glanced up. An enormous grizzly bear, 20 metres away, also turned around. Mark's eyes widened in shock. Grizzly and man fled from each other. Once Mark's hammering heart quietened, he remembered thinking it looked like a big, cuddly teddy. Days later, he saw a dead bear on the side of the road. Mark and Hana looked at its open jaw and saw teeth as big as fingers. Not so cuddly.

One afternoon they saw two bear cubs on the side of the road. They slowed to look at how cute they were. Then wondered where the mother was. Hana spotted her on the other side of the road. They had been told never to come between a mother and her cubs, and they were in the middle. With hearts racing, Hana and Mark took off fast.

In Wyoming, USA, a truck with snow chains stopped. An elk hunter leaned out of his truck window. 'No use carrying on with those. You won't get through.'

'Really?'

'Yep. Two feet of snow on the pass. We needed chains.'

But Mark and Hana weren't prepared to give up. At first, they rode along the truck's wheel tracks. But the higher they cycled, the thicker the snow was, until they were pushing their bikes through a metre of it. Down the other side, they used one leg as a tripod to balance their bike and help slow them down as they skidded on the hard-packed frozen snow. Around them, the conifer trees looked like a scene from a Christmas movie.

In mid-December, they crossed into New Mexico where adobe houses, weathered volcanoes and thorny cactus plants were the norm. On the dusty ground they saw a goose-stepping tarantula, and later a rattlesnake curled up. When they crept closer to take a photo, it reared up and scared them away.

One night in Mexico, they had gone to sleep in an abandoned building. Hana woke when she heard a mosquito buzzing. She turned on the torchlight and saw above their heads a scorpion – the size of

her hand – creeping towards them. She shook Mark awake. The scorpion scuttled further away. But not taking any chances, they set up their tent inside the building.

Some nights, it was difficult getting to sleep with coyotes howling outside. One evening, they heard an animal pacing around their tent. It howled and yipped. Was it a puma? They had seen tracks earlier that day. Any minute, they feared, the mountain lion would attack their tent. Mark unzipped the tent and peered out. Hana peeked behind him. A small, fluffy Andean fox snarled nearby. They'd camped in its territory, and it was most displeased.

On a hot and sweaty day, they reached a jungle river they had to cross. They took off most of their clothes and carried their bikes overhead, through deep water. As they emerged on the opposite bank, a man appeared. 'There are crocodiles in that river!' Luckily, they weren't that hungry that day!

On 7 September 2017, Hana woke with a jolt. An earthquake jolt. She'd experienced many growing up in Christchurch, so knew it was significant. For ninety seconds the hotel's concrete walls swayed and trembled. They hurriedly grabbed their gear. But the only way out of the building was down a stairwell in the middle of the building. They daren't risk getting trapped. When the shaking stopped, they rushed outside where frightened locals milled. Later they heard it was an 8.1-magnitude earthquake and 98 people had died in Southern Mexico.

Mark and Hana weren't in any rush to finish their trip. They spent a year in Peru, zigzagging back and forth over the remote Andes between Argentina and Chile. In March 2020, they heard chilling news: People were dying in China and then Italy from Covid. At first, they thought the pandemic wouldn't spread to South America. They were too far away, weren't they? But then a cruise ship docked in Patagonia in early March 2020, and when the tourists disembarked, they released Covid into the country. Within hours of the news breaking out, businesses closed. They didn't want tourists. The national parks and borders shut. The New Zealand Government urged New Zealanders to come home. **Hana and Mark rushed to Santiago airport. Twice they booked a plane home. Each time the airline cancelled it, as countries locked down. They queued for hours, hoping to get onto a standby flight. Then Santiago went into lockdown. The couple were stuck. After camping for two days at the airport, they boarded a plane, arriving in Auckland thirty-six hours before New Zealand went into lockdown. In 2022, the borders reopened, and they flew back to Chile to continue cycling to the bottom of South America, finishing in April 2023.**

PREPARING FOR YOUR OWN ADVENTURE

Perhaps you've dreamed of going on your own adventures. It might be:

- hiking in the mountains
- sailing on the sea
- flying to another country
- kayaking on a lake
- cycling down country lanes
- horse-riding on a long beach
- white-water rafting down a fast-moving river
- camping in the wilderness.

It is the adrenalin rush, not knowing what will happen next, and going outside our comfort zones that give us the thrill. Most of the time, these trips go without mishap. But occasionally, someone might fall, get lost or get stranded. Then a fun time can turn into a nightmare. The adventurers all prepared weeks, months, even years before taking off on their trip. They made sure they were fit, had safety gear with them and had plenty of food and water.

Here are some tips that might save your life:

HEALTH CHECKLIST	PACKING CLOTHES	PACKING ESSENTIALS
• Exercise beforehand. • Check whether you need to take any medications or have a vaccination. • If you have a medical condition such as asthma, take plenty of medication. • Before leaving, tell someone where you are going and when you plan to return.	• If somewhere hot, take loose-fitting clothes and a sun hat. • If somewhere cold, pack clothes you can layer on such as singlets, long-sleeved merino tops, jumpers and jackets plus a warm hat, gloves, socks. • Take an outer-layer jacket such as a windproof or rainproof coat.	• Torch • Waterproof matches or lighter • Whistle • Pocket knife • Compass • Cooking pan • Map • Mobile phone • Food • Water • Sun lotion

What is one of the most important items you need on your adventure? Guessed it? Water! If you run out of this precious stuff, you can collect it from nature. But start looking before you've run out.

- Collect rainwater – spread out a waterproof sheet on the ground. Peg it down with twigs and stretch it out just above the ground. A waterproof sheet could be your raincoat if you have nothing else.
- Collect dew – from cold surfaces or off leaves in the early morning.
- Follow animals to a stream or river. They are usually at the base of valleys.

What if you've found water, but you don't know if it is safe to drink? Filter it by pouring it through a clean sock or a nylon top. If you have camping cooking gear with you, boil the water for five minutes. Keep your water in the shade.

What should you do if you get lost? Keep positive, stay alert and take note of your surroundings. Never give up. Climb a hill or a high point and examine the surrounding land. It might help you find the easiest route out. Attract attention by:

- signalling with a mirror in bright sunlight
- leaving notes or signs for rescuers and marking your trail
- blowing on a whistle to alert searchers who are nearby
- moving your torch from left to right
- lighting a fire (but make sure it can't spread)
- making a huge SOS signal with sticks and stones
- phoning emergency services with your cell phone (you might have to climb to a high point to get reception).

It is always better to be prepared for the worst-case scenario rather than making decisions when you're scared or panicking. *Do you have what it takes to be an epic adventurer?*

Jean Batten's cat

FURTHER READING

Alaska to Patagonia by Mark Watson and Hana Black: www.highlux.co.nz
Ascend the Nile by Garth MacIntyre, Neil McGrigor and Cam McLeay (2009)
Jean Batten: The Garbo of the Skies by Ian Mackersey (1992)
Lydia Bradey: Going Up Is Easy by Lydia Bradey and Laurence Fearnley (2016): https://lydiabradey.com
One Girl One Dream by Laura Dekker (2018): https://lauradekkerworldsailingfoundation.com
Polar Dream: The First Solo Expedition by a Woman and Her Dog to the Magnetic North Pole by Helen Thayer (1993, 2001, 2013): www.helenthayer.com
Running Hot by Lisa Tamati and Nicola McCloy (2010): www.lisatamati.com
Sir Edmund Hillary: An Extraordinary Life by Alexa Johnston (2005)
The Dreamtime Voyage by Paul Caffyn (2010): https://paulcaffyn.co.nz
Waka by Matahi Whakataka-Brightwell (1994)

ABOUT THE AUTHORS

MARIA GILL fancies herself as an adventurer. She travelled with her family around Australia in a caravan, fossicking for gemstones and fishing in remote rivers when she was a teenager. From 19 years old, she rode a camel in Egypt, a donkey in Greece, an elephant in India and a bike in China. She's also sailed down the Nile River in a felucca. Nowadays, she travels New Zealand and Australian schools giving workshops and author talks. She's written sixty books over the last twenty years. Over that time, she's won the Supreme Book Award for *Anzac Heroes*, the Children's Choice Award (nonfiction) for *New Zealand Hall of Fame*, and eleven Storylines Notable Book Awards. In 2020, Storylines awarded Maria the Margaret Mahy Medal for services to children's literature. She also has a master's degree in creative writing, a journalism and a teaching degree. **www.mariagill.co.nz**

MARCO IVANCIC prefers playing soccer and exploring the world of computer games to travel. His ancestors once hailed from Croatia, but he has his feet firmly planted on Wellington soil. He's a ninja computer artist with a Massey University Illustration and Graphic Art degree (Honours). His favourite things to draw are action people and robots. He has illustrated seven books with Maria Gill. At the LIANZA awards, judges awarded him an Honourable Mention for the artwork in his first book, *New Zealand Sports Hall of Fame*. The second book, *Anzac Heroes*, won the Supreme Book Award, as well as the Nonfiction Award. His third, *Abel Tasman*, was a finalist for the Illustration Award at the New Zealand Children's & Young Adults' Book Awards. His sixth, *New Zealand Disasters*, was shortlisted in the 2021 national book awards. When he's not illustrating, he's drawing maps and designing book covers. **Marcoivancic.com**